D1074091

CARY
COMMUNITY ALLIES OF RAINBOW YOUTH

LOVE WITHOUT BOUNDS

An *IntersectionAllies* Book about Families

Written by Drs. Chelsea Johnson, LaToya Council, and Carolyn Choi

Illustrated by Ashley Seil Smith

dottir press
NEW YORK CITY

To Mimi, Bobos, and Lala

Published in 2023 by Dottir Press
33 Fifth Avenue
New York, NY 10003

Dottirpress.com

First printing January 2023
Production by Drew Stevens

Library of Congress Cataloging-in-Publication Data is available for this title.
ISBN 978-1-948340-51-9
eBook available
Manufactured in Canada by Prolific

A LETTER TO READERS

Dear Relatives:
Love without Bounds: An IntersectionAllies Book about Families celebrates the people we love and who love us.

Since there is no single type of family that is "normal" or "best," we use the word *families* instead of *family* to honor all the people who are important to us throughout our lives, as well as the infinite forms families take around the world. In these pages, you'll meet families created by chance and choice. You'll meet families of many sizes, cultures, and circumstances. Some families spend time together every day, while other families find ways to love each other across distance and time.

Love makes a family. And yet, social factors like identity, culture, and governments shape how family members show and experience love. Prisons, unjust laws, and national borders can separate parents from their children and families from their communities. Stigma and stereotypes can make people feel ashamed about who and how they love.

Love without Bounds asks that we respect other people's families as much as we do our own. After all, as people who share space on this earth, we are all in relation to one another all the time. We can be each other's chosen family by pushing for changes in our social systems to honor what we know to be true: love is love, and loving without bounds is a revolutionary act.

With love, we can make room for all!

From our family to yours,

—CLC Collective
aka Chelsea, LaToya, and Carolyn

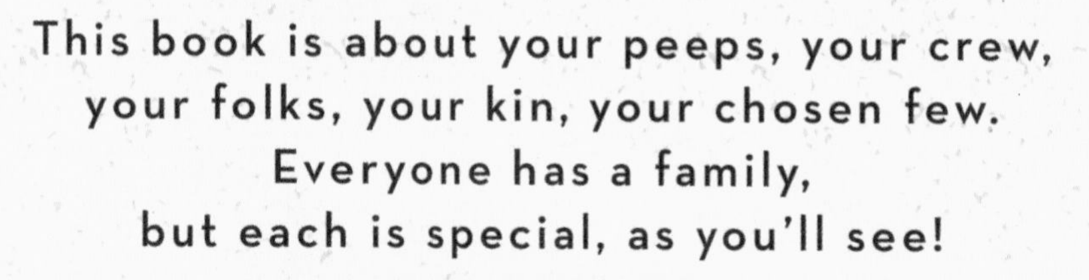

This book is about your peeps, your crew,
your folks, your kin, your chosen few.
Everyone has a family,
but each is special, as you'll see!

Yours and hers, his and theirs—
some big ol' groups, some tiny pairs.
No matter the size or situation,
it's love that serves as the foundation.

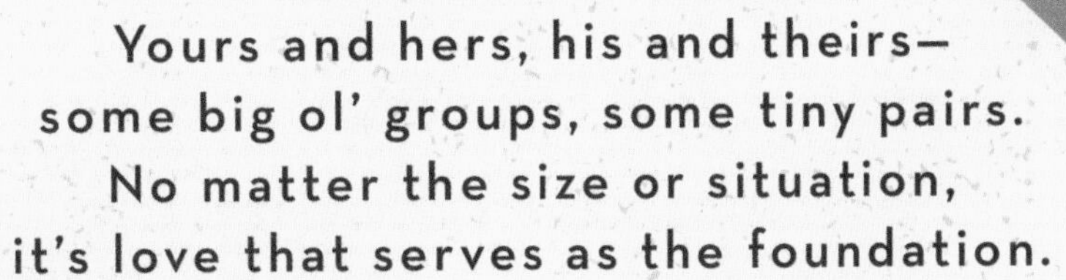

Some families include more than a few.
Some families are just teams of two.

Grown-ups and kids, moms and dads—
all families are lovely if love's what you add.

My fam is Mom, Mama, and me.
We are a "nuclear" family.

Mom sings me songs, Mama tucks me in.
I feel their love through the time we spend.

Our dearly beloveds have gathered today
to witness my parents' wedding day.

My wise abuela, my sneaky pet cat,
my out-of-town auntie (so fly in her hat!).

Friends who hug and primas who play,
siblings, uncles, and neighbors—hooray!

A joyous feast in celebration
of a family on the cusp of creation.

The beat of the music, laughter surrounds . . .

WE ARE A FAMILY!

WE LOVE WITHOUT BOUNDS!

My folks told me the coolest thing:
next year, I'll have a new sibling!

What will they like? How will they be?
Will everything change when it's not just me?

One thing's for sure: I'll do my part
and share the love that's in my heart.

And when the baby starts to grow,
I'll teach them everything I know!

Through thick and thin, through lows and highs,
siblings can be the best allies.

My sis was born in the Midwest,
but my life started with a quest.

Just like a vine joining a tree,
I was adopted into my family.

After praying and waiting and lots of wishing,
they welcomed me home—the piece they'd been missing!

Two family trees, one history.
My story is what makes me . . . *me*.

In my ***Loving*** family,
two legacies created me.

When flower buds start to appear,
our freedom holidays are here!

A Seder marks the start of spring . . .

. . . and on Juneteenth, we proudly sing,
LIFT EVERY VOICE AND SING 'TIL EARTH AND HEAVEN RING,
over barriers that made us hurt and hide
to this place where we can love with **pride**!

With each generation, our love compounds . . .

WE ARE A FAMILY!

WE LOVE WITHOUT

My nanay is just an ocean away
in a place I'd love to visit one day.
When the sun sets here for Grandma and me,
it's tomorrow across the big blue sea.

Ding-dong goes the sound of our video chats.
We goof off and giggle in our matching hats.

Some people might think that if a parent is gone,
their love and care has also moved on.

But the biggest love a parent can give
is a sacrifice so their family can live.

They deployed my dad to a faraway place,
miles from our home here on the base.

We watch the news both day and night.
I whisper, "Daddy, I hope you're all right."

We've got each other, but my whole family misses
the warmth of his hugs, the itch of his kisses.

We march and pray for the wars to cease,
so all of our families can live in peace.

"Congratulations! Come take your degree!
You've graduated from Ally Academy!"

So I move my tassel from left to right,
throw my hat in the air, and smile bright.

A bus ride away, in a distant town,
a big part of my world jumps up and down.

CERTIFICATE OF ACHIEVEMENT
AWARDED TO
Alicia Scott
ALLY ACADEMY

When I hear his voice, I wipe a tear.
Today was perfect, except I wish Dad was here.

He's my biggest cheerleader, and bottom line,
this achievement is his as much as it's mine.

Some families, like mine, change over time.
When my dads got married, our families combined.

My bonus dad came with kids of his own.
Who would've thought I'd miss playing alone?

But we circle 'round to share holiday fun.
Giving time, getting closer, together as one.

Families evolve. Who we love can too.
We cherish the old and welcome the new.

School days with Mom, weekends with Dad—
my parents made the best choice they had.

When they split, everything changed.
(In fact, my entire life rearranged.)

Boxes and toys, new apartments and houses,
new rules, new schools, and even new spouses.

But in choosing themselves, they both chose me.
We'll always be a family.

Sometimes, the family we're born into doesn't make us feel how we want to.

In these moments, our closest friends step in and help our hearts to mend . . .

a pen pal, a teammate, a snuggly pup—
those who care for you and build you up.

There's so much of life we can't control,
and our chosen family can make us whole.

There are times we must tell our loved ones goodbye,
and often too early, their souls meet the sky.

We honor the moments we spent together.
Through our memories, they live on forever.

With a keepsake or a walk to their resting place,
we remember their love, their laugh, their face.

Watching over us each day and night,
our ancestors are our guiding light.

So, what does *family* really mean?
They're the people who love us and make us feel seen,

the folks who give us time and care
by sharing with us and just being there.

A shoulder to lean on, a space to be free—
whoever gives us that is our family.

There's no perfect family form.
No family ever fits the norm.

Although bullies and laws can make us feel shame,
every family's important, and no two are the same.

In faraway places or right next to you,
those yet to be born and who've passed on too.

Growing and changing, together or apart,
your family are those who live in your heart.

To the loved ones we miss and the new kin we've found,

WE ARE A FAMILY!

WE LOVE WITHOUT BOUNDS!

LET'S LEARN TOGETHER

A *Love without Bounds* Discussion Guide

Families are made up of people who love one another and want the best for each other. Families can include people who are related, adopted, chosen, or just plain close to us. Parents, siblings, pets, cousins, grandparents, and friends are some of the many people that can make up a family. Some family members share a common **ancestor**, like a grandparent. Other family members meet each other throughout life, like romantic partners and friends. **Who is in your family? How does your family make you feel loved?**

Parents and children who share the same home make up what's called a **nuclear family**, like the one here that includes "Mom, Mama, and me." Nuclear families aren't all the same, and not everyone is part of a nuclear family. Lots of families are single-parent households with one parent and kid(s). Sometimes, neighbors, friends, and caregivers who are not related by blood contribute to a household. This is known as **community care**. Around the world, it is common to find children, parents, grandparents, and sometimes even great-grandparents living together under the same roof. Families are families because of the love they share, not their shape or size. **Were any families in this book like your family? How are they similar, and how are they different?**

A well-known Yoruba proverb says that "it takes a village to raise a child." One term to describe that village is **extended family**, which includes all of the relatives who don't live together under one roof. Extended families could be made up of cousins, aunts, uncles, grandparents, and even your cousins' cousins. Some extended families live near one another and can see each other all the time. Others live far apart and gather virtually or in person during happy occasions, like weddings, or sad moments, like funerals. **What moments bring your extended family together?**

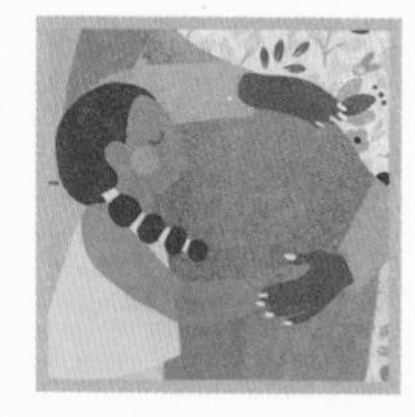

A **generation** is a group of people who were born around the same time as one another. Siblings are usually part of the same generation. Your parents might be one generation older than you, and your grandparents might be two generations older than you. **How many generations live in your home? How many generations of your family are alive today?**

Many families have **traditions** that are passed down from one generation to another. A tradition is something meaningful you do together again and again. Some traditions are cultural, others are religious, and others are just for fun, like a family movie night each Saturday. The family on this page is celebrating **Passover**, a Jewish holiday that honors the Hebrew people's escape and liberation from slavery in Egypt. They are also celebrating **Juneteenth** or **Black Independence Day**, when the last group of enslaved Black Americans in Galveston, Texas, finally received news that they were legally free—over two years after the Emancipation Proclamation was issued in 1863. During Passover, families hold a Seder feast with foods that symbolize and help retell the story of their ancestors' Exodus from Egypt. During Juneteenth, families often hold picnics, parades, and cookouts to rejoice in freedom and community. **What is your favorite family tradition? What does this ritual say about your family's values and beliefs?**

The phrase "Lift every voice and sing till earth and heaven ring" comes from the "**Negro National Anthem,**" written by Black American poet and activist James Weldon Johnson in 1900. This iconic song eventually became a rallying cry for the civil rights movement and continues to serve as a reminder of the pain, determination, faith, and triumph that characterize the Black American experience.

Families must deal with policies and laws created by governments. Sometimes laws can be racist, sexist, and homophobic toward families. ***Loving*** on this page is capitalized and italicized in honor of Mildred Loving, an African American and Native American woman, and Richard Loving, her white husband, who were sentenced to prison for violating Virginia's Racial Integrity Act. These brave spouses challenged their case, ***Loving v. Virginia***, all the way up to the US Supreme Court, which in 1967 decided that state laws banning interracial marriage were illegal. It took another forty-eight years for the US Supreme Court to recognize LGBTQ+ marriages through ***Obergefell v. Hodges***. The word **pride** is on this page in honor of that important moment for LGBTQ+ families.

Adoption is when an adult makes a legal commitment to care for someone. Sometimes, grandparents adopt grandkids, or aunts and uncles adopt nieces, nephews, or niblings. And sometimes, community members adopt each other. Other times, adoptees join their families from different cultures or parts of the world. These experiences show that love is bigger and more powerful than being related by blood, being from the same place, or the challenges that life may bring.

The Doyle family lives in the American Midwest and adopted one of their children from South Korea. This is a type of **international adoption**, meaning the adoptive parents and the adopted child are from different countries. International adoption from Korea to the US was common during and after the Korean War (1950–1953). This time period is an important part of Asian American history because it began before the Immigration and Nationality Act of 1965, a law that ended limits to the number of nonwhite immigrants who could come to the US. Over the next few decades, international adoption challenged many Americans' understanding of love across race, culture, and difference during a time when many communities were impacted by racial segregation.

Many of our characters have experienced **family separation**. Families who live apart in different countries are called **transnational families**. In this scene, our narrator video chats with their mother, who is working abroad. **Are you or anyone you know part of a transnational family? What are the different ways you can connect and catch up with loved ones who live far from you? Can you describe one way you can show care and love across distance?**

The military works for the government, but it's made up of everyday people like our family, friends, and neighbors. When a soldier is **deployed**, or sent to places where there is military action, their whole family is affected, and everyone makes sacrifices. Military service or living in a war zone can mean that families face harm, experience uncertainty, and get separated from one another. That's why some military experiences inspire antiracist, feminist, decolonial, environmental, and peace work like clearing out land mines, participating in street protests, sharing antiwar education in schools, and advocating for mental health support.

DISCUSSION GUIDE CONTINUED

Sometimes the people we love are accused of breaking the law. When that happens, they may be imprisoned, detained, or jailed by the government, which separates them from their families. While we don't often talk about it, many kids grow up knowing a parent, sibling, grandparent, relative, or family friend who is or has been incarcerated. No matter who the loved one is, **incarceration** is hard for everyone involved and can leave those left behind feeling like they are "doing time together," as sociologist Dr. Megan Comfort says. Incarceration can create challenges for families, like making time for faraway visits, not being able to communicate easily, speaking up for an incarcerated loved one's well-being, or rushing to help them find a job upon release. Even though it may take extra work, family members and friends try their best to support one another.

Prison abolitionists, like Dr. Angela Davis, work to create a society that doesn't rely on prisons, policing, or detention to help heal and move forward from people's actions. Others, like the American Civil Liberties Union (ACLU), work to make the justice system more fair and to reduce the burdens of incarceration on families and communities. **How can you support friends and family members who are incarcerated or impacted by a loved one's incarceration? How might we encourage healing and taking responsibility for one's actions without prisons?**

Families change and evolve over time. One type of family change is **marriage**, when adults make a formal promise to join their lives together as **spouses**. Another family change is the addition or birth of a new family member. On this page, the Smiths and the Lins are becoming a **blended family**, which is when adults with kids move in together and their families combine.

Separation or **divorce**, when spouses decide not to be romantic partners anymore, is another type of family change. Families can sometimes find new ways to love and respect one another after separation or divorce. For example, some parents continue to share the responsibility of taking care of their children after separating, like the Chois. This is called **co-parenting**.

Sociologists (like the three of us!) use the terms **chosen family** and **fictive kin** to describe family members who are not related by blood or through marriage but choose to support, love, and care for each other anyway. Fictive kin can include godparents, neighbors, roommates, foster or adoptive family, close friends, and house parents in LGBTQ+ families. Chosen families can be important support systems during hard times, like when relatives disagree, live far away, or pass on. The authors of this book consider themselves a chosen family because we have relied on each other to make it through tough times. **Who is your chosen family? How did you meet?**

The **death** of a family member is another way families change. If you've experienced the loss of someone you love, you are not alone. When someone we love dies, we may feel many things, like surprise, sadness, or gratitude. All emotions are okay. Feeling our feelings together can be helpful, especially while doing things like gathering at funerals, places of worship, or in our homes to share stories about loved ones we've lost. It can be comforting to know that, like all the plants and animals around us, we are part of an endless circle of life—birthing, growing, passing on, and becoming a nurturing source for other living beings to thrive.

Ancestors are the people in a family who came before you and your living family members but have passed away. The actions, hopes, and dreams of your ancestors are forever alive in you because their choices and values made your life possible. Many cultures around the world believe that ancestors remain connected to the living world and seek their ancestors' guidance, wisdom, and support through prayers or offerings that commemorate them. Día de los Muertos in Mexico, Qingming in China, Chuseok in the Koreas, All Saints' Day in Europe, and the Egungun festival in Nigeria are all moments where families celebrate and remember loved ones who've passed. **Ask a family member to share a favorite memory of an ancestor with you. Write down what you learn to start your family archive and keep the memory of your ancestors strong.**

Big or unexpected family changes can be overwhelming. If this happens to you, find a trusted adult to talk to about your feelings. Taking care of your mental, emotional, spiritual, and physical wellness is called **self-care**. Self-care looks different for everyone, but in general, it means taking time to stop, think, and do something that brings you joy, rest, and balance. Some common self-care activities include reading, journaling, making art, exercising, or spending time in nature. **What does self-care look like for you?**

Did you know that the idea of self-care came from women of color feminist activists? Many women of color have had to advocate to be included in laws and conversations led by more powerful groups in society. They've done so by protesting, writing letters to politicians, and creating support services for people in their communities. This work is important . . . but tiring! Self-care can help give activists the energy to continue their push for change. As Black lesbian feminist activist Audre Lorde explains, "Caring for myself is not self-indulgence. It is self-preservation." **Self-preservation** means you protect yourself from harm. So, as you work to "make room for all," don't forget to take care of yourself!

Now let's put self-care into practice.

This book brings up big topics that can provoke big feelings. Perhaps a story reminded you of your own relatives or a friend's family. **Honor whatever feelings you had when reading this book. Take a moment to recognize how you feel right now. How can you give yourself the love and care you deserve?**

ABOUT THE AUTHORS

Dr. Chelsea Johnson (she/her/hers)

I grew up in a nuclear family, the youngest of the "kiddies three." My extended family lived a road trip's distance from our home in Illinois. I looked forward to Easter, when Grandma Mildred would make her famous mac and cheese, and the Saturday before Christmas, when I'd learn about my cousins' new friends over a plate of fried rice. When I think of family, I also think of my Soul Sistahs, my Spelman sisters, and my CLC sisters—a chosen family of strong women who have protected my heart through bullies, breakups, and big life changes. Sisterhood is part of what brought me to feminism and inspired my research and writing on Black women's activism and beauty cultures as well as my research in tech, which centers how to design for trust and safety on the internet. When I'm not researching or writing, you're most likely to find me snuggled up with the latest evolution of my family—my husband Jonathan, Bichpoo Lala, and a baby on the way.

Dr. LaToya Council (she/her/hers)

I grew up in a mother-headed household with my older sister, Sabrina. My father died when I was three, and my mother died three months into my college experience at Spelman. Sometimes, when I think about my parents, I feel sad because my sister and I are having new and exciting adventures and they're not here to experience them with us. When I feel that way, I find comfort in knowing my sweet grandmother, aunties, uncles, and many cousins are a phone call away, listening to me and reminiscing about my ancestors. I also have friends who are family. My nuclear family is small, but my extended family is abundant. Now I'm a professor studying Black middle-class families and their experiences with work, life, and self-care practices. When I'm not researching and teaching, you'll find me at a cool coffee shop, learning about coffee, baking something sweet, diving into a good book, or hanging with my cat, Mimi.

Dr. Carolyn Choi (she/her/hers)

I grew up in a mother-headed household with my younger sister. The tightness of our little family made it feel like we were three sisters learning together, encouraging one another, and sharing care work. Through the ups and downs of life, my omma (mom), sister, and I continue to be each other's rocks, confidants, and best friends. More recently, I've reconnected with my apa (father), who is currently undergoing treatment for his health. As an adult, I've created a chosen family that includes my partner and a medley of fur friends. My pug, Mr. Bobos, is my truest companion. His little siblings—Gogi, a fellow pug, and Soondae, a spirited pit bull puppy—make my house a home. My family's story of immigration from Korea to Koreatown, Los Angeles, inspires my work as a researcher on international migration, as well as one of my favorite ways to spend downtime: playing pansori, a form of Korean folk music.

Ashley Seil Smith (she/her/hers)

I grew up in a nuclear family of five daughters, sharing the title of "youngest" with my identical twin sister. In college, I studied anthropology, where I witnessed many different forms of family and kinship around the world. Today, my family also includes my husband and the many beloved animals we've brought in over the years, including our three dogs, Shoji, Penny, and Frankie. My sisters—whether from birth or chosen—will always be some of the most important people in my life. I'm grateful for the family I was born into, the family I've created, and the endless diversity of families around the world.

BIBLIOGRAPHY

Van Gulden — Rabb-Bartels
REAL PARENTS, REAL CHILDREN
Parenting the Adopted Child

ARRESTED JUSTICE: BLACK WOMEN, VIOLENCE, AND AMERICA'S PRISON NATION
Beth E. Richie

ARE PRISONS OBSOLETE?
Angela Davis

AN ABOLITIONIST'S HANDBOOK
PATRISSE CULLORS

TURNING THE BEAT AROUND
Lesbian Parenting 1986
AUDRE LORDE

Avila Hondagneu-Sotelo
"I'M HERE, BUT I'M THERE"
The Meanings of Latina Transnational Motherhood

Beth E. Richie
COMPELLED TO CRIME
The Gender Entrapment of Battered Black Women

Michael Messner
UNCONVENTIONAL COMBAT
Intersectional Action in the Veterans' Peace Movement

ALL ABOUT LOVE
NEW VISIONS
bell hooks

Dawn M. Dow
MOTHERING WHILE BLACK
Boundaries and Burdens of Middle-Class Parenthood

CHILDREN OF GLOBALIZATION
Rhacel Parreñas

THE TIES THAT BIND
Timeless Values for African American Families
JOYCE LADNER

BONNIE THORNTON DILL
ACROSS THE BOUNDARIES OF RACE AND CLASS:
An Exploration of Work and Family Among Black Female Domestic Servants

INVISIBLE FAMILIES
Gay Identities, Relationships, and Motherhood Among Black Women
Mignon R. Moore

Maxine Baca Zinn
FAMILY, FEMINISM, AND RACE IN AMERICA

Doméstica
Immigrant Workers Cleaning and Caring in the Shadows of Affluence
Hondagneu-Sotelo

BLACK INTIMACIES
A Gender Perspective on Families and Relationships
Shirley A. Hill

DOING TIME TOGETHER
Love and Family in the Shadow of the Prison
Megan Comfort

Sacrificing Families
NAVIGATING LAWS, LABOR, AND LOVE ACROSS BORDERS
Leisy J. Abrego